Let's Be Friends

Created & Written by MISTY TAGGART
Illustrated by KAREN BELL

WORD PUBLISHING
Dallas·London·Vancouver·Melbourne

Behind the third cloud to the right,
just around the corner from the rainbow, is the Angel Academy.
This is where young angels learn to be real guardian angels.

Text © 1995 by Susan Misty Taggart. Illustrations © 1995 by Karen Bell.

Trademark application has been filed on the following: The Angel Academy ™, StarCentral™,
Angel Heaven™, Jubilate™, Mirth™, Angelus™, Stella the Starduster™, Astrid™, Staria™, Miss Celestial™, Puffaluff™.

Managing Editor: Laura Minchew   *Project Editor:* Beverly Phillips

Library of Congress Cataloging-in-Publication Data

Taggart, Misty, 1940–
    Let's be friends/created and written by Misty Taggart;
illustrated by Karen Bell.
        p.   cm. (The angel academy; #5)
    "Word kids!"
    Summary: Two angels-in-training get a difficult assignment when they are sent to help a girl learn how to be a good
friend after her family moves.
    ISBN 0-8499-5084-8 (pbk.)
    [1. Guardian angels—Fiction. 2. Angels—Fiction. 3. Friendship—Fiction. 4. Moving, Household—Fiction.] I. Bell, Karen,
1949– ill. II. Title III. Series: Taggart, Misty, 1940– Angel academy; #5.
PZ7.T1284Co 1995
[E]—dc20
                                                                                            94-45102
                                                                                                CIP
                                                                                                AC

Printed in the United States of America   95 96 97 **98** 99 00 LBM 9 8 7 6 5 4 3 2 1

STARIA

She thinks she's very grown-up, but don't you believe it.

ASTRID

Her laugh is as big as her sweet tooth.

ANGELUS

If you have a question about anything, he has the answer—he thinks.

JUBILATE

He's ready to right every wrong—and has a lot of fun doing it.

MIRTH

She may be small, but she can be big trouble.

"I won't go!" The short, rather skinny little eight-year-old was very determined. She pushed her big glasses up on her freckled nose.

The orange moving truck was packed. Her mother and little brother were already in the minivan. But Cookie stood her ground, holding tightly to her dog, Firecracker. Cookie didn't want to move to a new neighborhood.

"Honey, you'll like the new house." Her father smiled as he slid the van door open.

At last, Cookie and Firecracker climbed in, and the Moore family headed for their new neighborhood.

When they arrived, Cookie had to admit the new house was nice. There were even kids riding bikes and playing jump rope next-door. But Cookie was too shy to go over and meet them.

"What if they don't like me?" Cookie asked
her mom. Some of the kids in the old
neighborhood had called Cookie names because
she wore glasses. It hurt Cookie's feelings. She
wanted things to be different here. She hoped
she'd have lots of friends.

In Angel Heaven, Miss Celestial's class had just finished their Meteor Math lesson. As usual, Angelus got a perfect score.

"All you do is study," Astrid said. "What about having fun?"

"Learning *is* fun," Angelus replied.

"It's sort of nerdy, if you ask me," said Jubilate.

Mirth giggled. Miss Celestial reminded them it wasn't nice to make fun of each other.

The final bell rang and Jubilate hurried for the door. But he slid to a stop as Miss Celestial's StarCom pin started blinking. School wasn't quite over, after all.

Jedediah the Operator of StarCentral was on his way to The Angel Academy with an Earth Assignment.

When Jedediah arrived, he told the class all
about Cookie, Firecracker, and the big move.

"Wow! Look at that terrific dog!" exclaimed
Jubilate when he saw Firecracker. "Do you think
the Archangel would let me have a dog, Miss
Celestial?"

Miss Celestial laughed. "I don't know. But, I'm
sure you and Firecracker will be good buddies."

Jubilate leaped into the air with excitement.
"I'm heading for Earth. Yippee!"

Miss Celestial chose Staria to go with him. Happily, the two guardian angels-in-training disappeared into the billowy clouds as they slid down The Big Cloud Slide to Earth.

Back on Earth, Cookie was looking for Firecracker. "Now where is that dog?"

"Look," giggled Staria. "He's next-door trying to squeeze through their doggie door."

Who said that? Cookie hadn't seen anyone come into her yard.

"Up here!" shouted Jubilate. He was hanging upside down from the branch of a big elm tree. Staria was sitting next to him.

Cookie thought it was the new neighbor kids playing tricks on her. She tugged at Staria's wings trying to prove they weren't real.

"Ouch!" cried Staria.

"They *are* real!" exclaimed Cookie.

When Jubilate and Staria finished telling Cookie all about Angel Heaven and The Angel Academy, Cookie was very excited.

"This is great," she giggled. "My own angels!"

The next morning was Cookie's first day in her
new school. She had been scared to go. But now, two
angels would be going with her.

On the way to school, Firecracker chased Jubilate.
Each time the dog was about to catch him, the angel
would fly up into the air. *"WOOF! WOOF!"* barked
Firecracker.

Staria laughed. "I think he wants to fly, too."

A neighbor girl ran to catch up with Cookie. "Hi, I'm Lissy," she said.

"Hi," said Cookie. "Wanna walk to school with us?"

Lissy giggled. "Silly. Your dog can't go to school!"

Cookie had forgotten that only she and Firecracker could see or hear the two angels-in-training.

Lissy was taller and a year older than Cookie—but the two girls were in the same grade. Cookie liked Lissy and hoped they could be friends.

The playground was filled with laughing children. "Watch this," said Jubilate as he jumped into the middle of a game of kickball.

"Hey! What's going on?" yelled one of the little boys, as their ball seemed to be darting about on its own. They had no idea they were playing kickball with an angel!

Cookie and Lissy were swinging when a little boy began shouting, "Can't read! Can't write! Lissy isn't very bright!" Other children joined in. Tears filled Lissy's eyes.

Now Cookie understood why Lissy was still in the same grade. She had trouble learning.

A few days later, a girl at school told Cookie not to play with Lissy if she wanted to have any other friends."

"That would be a mean thing to do," said Staria. "Don't listen to her, Cookie."

Cookie did like Lissy. But no matter what her angels-in-training said . . . she had to pretend Lissy wasn't her friend. Cookie didn't want to be teased, too, not at her new school.

That afternoon, Cookie ran straight home. Jubilate and Staria flew behind.

"Hey, wait up!" called Jubilate.

"You forgot to wait for Lissy." Staria hoped Cookie would change her mind and still be friends with Lissy.

But Cookie kept on running. "Let her find another friend."

Staria was very disappointed in Cookie.

"Please don't do this," Staria said. "You'll hurt Lissy's feelings."

"I thought you were *my* angels, not Lissy's," Cookie said. "Why don't you go back to Angel Heaven!" Then she ran to her room to work on her dinosaur project.

"What are we going to do?" sighed Staria. "Cookie won't talk to us, and Lissy's feelings are hurt."

"Yeah, I sure wish we could ask Miss Celestial what to do," Jubilate added.

Later that night, Cookie saw that her angels were still there. "Go away!" she shouted. Then Cookie jumped into bed and refused to talk to them.

But Staria and Jubilate didn't go away. They had come to help Cookie, and that's what they would do—somehow.

Staria reminded Cookie, "Lissy needs a friend. She needs you."

Cookie didn't want to listen. She plugged her ears with her fingers and hummed as loudly as she could!

The next morning, Cookie ran off to school. When she reached the corner, Jubilate and Staria were waiting for her.

"Leave me alone!" Cookie said.

Then she saw Lissy carefully carrying her own dinosaur project to school. Lissy was very proud because she had finished it a day early. "Hi, Cookie," she called.

Why did Lissy have to be so nice? Cookie looked right past her angels and stubbornly started teasing Lissy. "Can't read! Can't write!"

Lissy began to cry. She turned to run away. But she didn't see Firecracker until it was too late—*OOPS!* Lissy tripped over the big dog, and the dinosaur went flying!

"Catch it, Jubilate!" called Cookie! He tried, but the dinosaur hit the sidewalk and broke into a million pieces!

On the playground after school, Jubilate and Staria tried to cheer up a very sad Cookie. She was happy they were still there. "I'm so sorry for what I did."

"Then go tell Lissy," said Staria.

A big smile filled Cookie's face. "Thanks, I will!" she called as she rushed to catch up with her friend. "Hey, Lissy, wait for me!"

As Staria and Jubilate returned to Angel Heaven, they looked back to see the two friends walking home together.

A few days later, Miss Celestial was handing out grades for the spelling test. "You did very well, Mirth," she said.

"Angelus studied with me," she said proudly.

Jubilate could see Earth from the classroom window. "Come look at Lissy!" he called. All the angels-in-training rushed to see.

"Lissy's dinosaur science project won a prize," Staria exclaimed.

"But I thought it was broken," Astrid said.

"Cookie helped her make a new one," Staria proudly replied.

Jubilate and Staria had successfully completed their Earth Assignment. And that day, everyone in Miss Celestial's Angel Academy class agreed that Cookie had learned to be a good friend.

Look for these and other ANGEL ACADEMY™ books and products

at your favorite bookstore, gift shop, and retailer:

Sister,
Stay
Out!

Angel Parade
Pileup

The Staria Dress-Up Set
With Book
by Daval International, LTD.

The
Razzleberry
Rescue

The Angel Academy:
A Collection of Modern
Angel Tales

Don't miss the fun! Join THE ANGEL ACADEMY™ KIDS CLUB.

A one-year membership includes a Welcome Packet of fun sent directly from Angel Heaven. You'll get a Club Membership I.D. Card, Angel Academy Surprises and Special Offers throughout the year, and a special Birthday Surprise!

Do not tear out this page from your book. Photocopy the form below or use a clean sheet of paper and PRINT the following information:

Child's Name: _____ Girl ❏ Boy ❏

Address: _____

City: _____ State: _____ ZIP: _____

Phone: (_____) _____ Age: _____ Birthdate: _____

For a one-year membership, send the completed registration form along with a check or money order for $10.00, per child, ($13.00 in Canada) to:

THE ANGEL ACADEMY™ KIDS CLUB
P.O. Box 39480
Membership Dept.
Phoenix, AZ 85069–9480

Please allow 6–8 weeks for delivery. Subject to change without notice. AZ residents add sales tax.

The Angel Academy Kids Club is a division of Estee Productions, Inc.